TYRANNOSAURUS REX VS. EDNA

THE VERY FIRST CHICKEN

DOUGLAS REES

illustrated by JED HENRY

Henry Holt and Company

NEW YORK

Tyrannosaurus stomped through the forest. He roared. He gnashed. He cried,

"I am Tyrannosaurus Rex and I want breakfast!"

Triceratops heard him and
ran away as fast as she could.
"Run," she cried to Ankylosaurus.
"Tyrannosaurus Rex is coming!"

Ankylosaurus ran, too.
"**Scram!**" she shouted
to Parasaurolophus.

"Tyrannosaurus
is looking for
breakfast!"

They all ran past Edna, the very first chicken.

"What's up?" she asked.

"Get out of here, you strange-looking little whatever-you-are," Parasaurolophus said.

"Or Tyrannosaurus will eat you right up."

Edna didn't run. She just stayed where she was, pecking seeds for her breakfast.

When Tyrannosaurus saw Edna, he roared,
"I am **Tyrannosaurus**, lord of the forest.
Beware my mighty claws and terrible jaws."
"I am Edna the chicken," said Edna.

"Beware my mighty beak
and terrible flapping wings."

Tyrannosaurus roared again.

"Beware my deadly stomp and long, sharp teeth."

"Beware my pointy claws and many feathers," said Edna.

"I am **big** and **fierce** and you should be afraid of me," Tyrannosaurus said.

"I am **small** and **brave**

and **YOU** should be afraid of **me**,"

Edna told him.

Tyrannosaurus
gobbled her up
in one
bite.

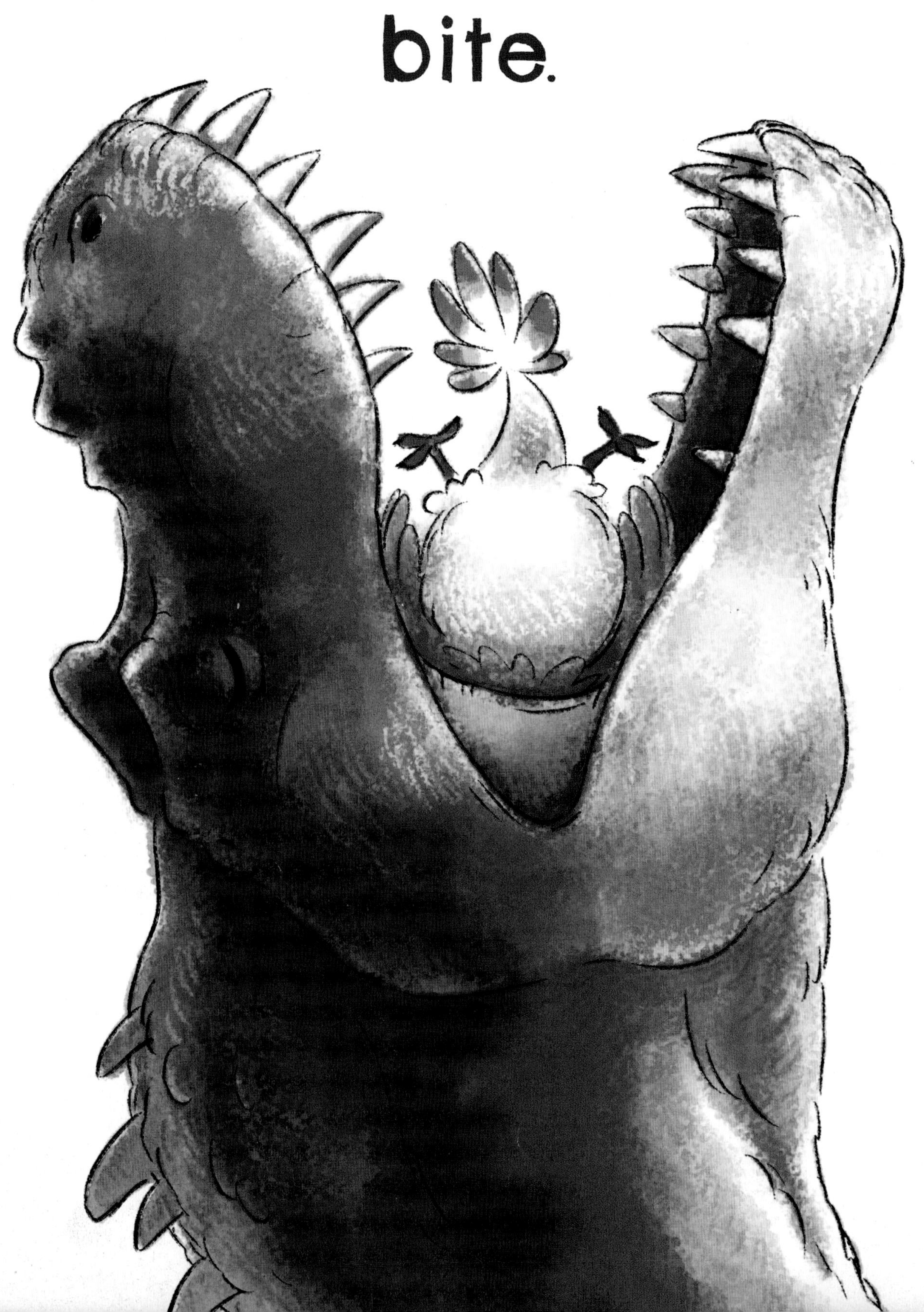

It was dark in Tyrannosaurus's mouth. It smelled **terrible**.

Edna grabbed Tyrannosaurus's tongue with her pointy claws.

Tyrannosaurus roared a new roar. "OW! Et o of y ongue."

Edna hung on tight.

Edna pecked.

"Ee-YOW!" screamed Tyrannosaurus.

"Et out of y outh!"

Edna flapped her wings
till her feathers flew.

"Ughk. Oookh. Eegh.
Ah-ah-ah-ah,"
gasped Tyrannosaurus.

That sneeze blew Edna
out of his mouth, soaring
across the forest . . .

. . . and straight into a giant redwood.

Tyrannosaurus tried to roar.
Feathers came out.
Tyrannosaurus tried again.
"I am Ahanasawus Ex,"
he said.
"I am ing of the orest."

Edna ruffled up her feathers. She flapped her wings. She stretched out her neck and clucked her loudest

Tyrannosaurus turned and ran.
Edna flapped down to the ground

and chased him.

They ran through trees and over flowers.

They ran across streams
and up hills.

Every dinosaur in the
forest saw them.

Finally Tyrannosaurus ran right
out of the forest and out of sight.
He didn't get breakfast that day.

"Thank you," said Parasaurolophus and Triceratops and Ankylosaurus.

"You are **awesome**."

"You are welcome," said Edna.

After that, Edna protected the other dinosaurs. Tyrannosaurus **never** came back.

Which is why today there
are no Tyrannosaurus Rexes
but plenty of chickens.

AUTHOR'S NOTE

There were no fights between Tyrannosauruses and chickens, but birds and dinosaurs did live during the same time period. In fact, birds are so closely related to dinosaurs like Tyrannosaurus rex and Allosaurus that scientists now believe birds are living dinosaurs. Some of the fiercest dinosaurs, like Velociraptor, had feathers. Did T. rex have feathers? We don't know—but it's possible. He and Edna were very close relatives.

For Carol Wolf
—D. R.

For Mei-Mei
—J. H.

Henry Holt and Company, *Publishers since 1866*
175 Fifth Avenue, New York, New York 10010
mackids.com

Library of Congress Cataloging-in-Publication Data is available.
ISBN 978-1-62779-510-4

Our books may be purchased in bulk for promotional, educational, or business use. Please contact your local bookseller or the Macmillan Corporate and Premium Sales Department at (800) 221-7945 ext. 5442 or by e-mail at MacmillanSpecialMarkets@macmillan.com.

First Edition—2017 / Designed by April Ward

The artist used scanned pencil and watercolor textures combined with digital watercolor techniques in Adobe Photoshop to create the illustrations for this book.

Printed in China by Hung Hing Off-set Printing Co. Ltd., Heshan City, Guangdong Province

1 3 5 7 9 10 8 6 4 2